Michael and Jane Pelusey

THE MEDIA

Internet

CHELSEA HOUSE
PUBLISHERS
A Haights Cross Communications ✦ Company ®

Philadelphia

This edition first published in 2006 in the United States of America by Chelsea House Publishers, a subsidiary of Haights Cross Communications.

A Haights Cross Communications ✦ Company ®

All rights reserved. No part of this publication may be reproduced or transmitted in any form or by any means without the written permission of the publisher.

Chelsea House Publishers
2080 Cabot Boulevard West, Suite 201
Langhorne, PA 19047-1813

The Chelsea House world wide web address is www.chelseahouse.com

First published in 2005 by
MACMILLAN EDUCATION AUSTRALIA PTY LTD
627 Chapel Street, South Yarra 3141

Visit our website at www.macmillan.com.au

Associated companies and representatives throughout the world.

Library of Congress Cataloging-in-Publication Data applied for.
ISBN 0 7910 8803 0

Edited by Anne Löhnberg and Angelique Campbell-Muir
Text and cover design by Ivan Finnegan, iF Design
All photographs and images used in design © Pelusey Photography.
Cover photograph: Students learning to use the Internet, courtesy of Pelusey Photography.

Printed in China

Acknowledgments
Michael and Jane Pelusey would like to thank Eva Brett of Virtual Synchronicity, Terry and Angela of NetFX and June Horner.
The publisher is grateful to the following for permission to reproduce copyright material:

All photographs courtesy of Pelusey Photography.

While every care has been taken to trace and acknowledge copyright, the publisher tenders their apologies for any accidental infringement where copyright has proved untraceable. Where the attempt has been unsuccessful, the publisher welcomes information that would redress the situation.

CONTENTS

When a word is printed in **bold**, you can look up its meaning in the glossary on page 31.

THE MEDIA

People communicate in many different ways. One thing common to all forms of communication is that a message is conveyed. Communicating is about spreading information and sharing it with others, in spoken and written words as well as in pictures.

The different means we use to communicate are called media. Each of them is designed to spread information and news, entertain people, or let them share experiences. The audience can be one person or a million. Forms of communication that reach millions of people at the same time are called mass media. They include:

◎ the Internet
◎ film and television
◎ magazines
◎ newspapers
◎ photography
◎ radio.

The media have great influence in our everyday lives. They inform us about current events, expose us to advertising, and entertain us.

Media play an important role in a family's life.

4

THE INTERNET

The Internet is a world-wide computer-based system for the spreading of information. It is a relatively new medium that allows us to communicate instantly with people all over the world. On the Internet we can read the news, do research for a hobby, play games, go shopping, and send messages to other people. Although the technology is rather new, it is used by millions of people around the world.

A world-wide computer network

The Internet works by linking millions of computers that are a long way away from each other. All these computers are connected by telephone lines and other cables to form a network.

To get onto the Internet, a computer sends signals via the connection to an **Internet service provider (ISP)**. The signals arrive at a **server**. The server is connected to other cables that give it access to computers all around the world.

Cables connecting computers at an Internet service provider

EARLY INTERNET

A computer was operated over a telephone line for the first time in 1940. However, the Internet as a realistic idea began in the 1960s, and it only really took off in the 1990s.

In 1962, the military defense forces of the United States were spread around the world. They wanted a faster, more efficient way to communicate between departments. Scientists were given the job of designing a new communication system. The Advanced Research Projects Agency (ARPA) came up with a system called ARPANET. In 1972, this system was demonstrated to the public for the first time at a computer conference. In 1986, ARPA established the categories of **domain names** used today.

Researchers at universities developed the system further and used it to communicate with each other. They invented ways to send letters (electronic mail, or e-mail), chat and have **online** conferences. The first e-mail **software** was created in 1972 by Ray Tomlinson. He was responsible for putting the @ symbol in e-mail addresses.

NEWS FLASH

DOMAIN NAMES
The domain categories chosen by ARPA include:

◎ **.com or .co** commercial
◎ **.edu**　　　 educational
◎ **.net**　　　 network
◎ **.org**　　　 organization

Modern Internet

Today, the Internet has become a global form of communication. Anyone who has access to a computer with a **modem** and telephone line at home, school, or work can connect to it. Technological developments allow people to have more than one Internet connection in their own home.

Many businesses have become dependent on the Internet for communicating, ordering products, and banking.

Millions of people throughout the **developed world** are communicating and sharing information almost instantly via the Internet. In less-developed countries, many people do not have access to the expensive equipment needed to take advantage of the Internet. Although in most countries there are places where people can go to use Internet technology, billions of people are missing out on this communication revolution.

In India, many people do not have computers at home, but Internet access is available in shops.

Students in many countries learn to use the Internet.

PARTS OF THE INTERNET

There are many different parts to the Internet.

Internet service providers

An Internet service provider, or ISP, is a company with big, fast computers that are connected to the Internet at all times. Computers in homes, businesses, and schools connect to an ISP via telephone lines to gain access to the Internet.

File transfer

Files can be transferred from one computer to another by a method called file transfer protocol (FTP). Computers use FTP to **download** files from the Internet.

E-mail

The most-used part of the Internet is electronic mail (e-mail). Anyone with an e-mail address can send and receive messages, pictures, and files in seconds. People use e-mail to send information around the world quickly and cheaply.

Messages and pictures are sent around the world via e-mail.

NEWS FLASH

E-MAIL ADDRESSES

Each e-mail address is unique. For example, **jsmith@supernet.co.uk** is made up of:
- a username **jsmith**
- the symbol for "at" **@**
- the name of the ISP **supernet**
- a domain abbreviation **co**
- an abbreviation for the country **uk**.

The United States of America does not have a country abbreviation.

The World Wide Web

The World Wide Web (www, "the Web") connects millions of computers within the Internet. It is made up of millions of different Websites that link to each other.

WEBSITES

Websites are a bit like magazines on the Internet. They are created by people who want to tell others about their ideas, products, or information. The front page of a Website is called the home page. Each Website has its own address, called a Uniform Resource Locator (URL).

THE BROWSER

You need a computer program called a browser to **surf the Web**. There are many different browsers, such as Netscape® and Internet Explorer.

PORTALS AND SEARCH ENGINES

Some Websites, called portals, are set up especially to direct people to other Websites. Other Websites, called search engines, allow people to search the Web. Users can type in keywords, and the search engine then displays a list of Websites that may interest them.

CHATTING

Some Websites and special software allow many people on computers to communicate with each other at the same time. Friends, family members, and even strangers can "chat" by typing to each other in **real time**.

Chatting with a friend

WORKING ON THE INTERNET

Many people are involved in the Internet business. Often, they come from a computer background. They have developed Internet skills over time or have taken classes to learn how to do the work.

The Internet service provider

Internet service providers employ lots of people. Many of them are computer experts, who work to keep the servers running as smoothly as possible. Other people help customers with their Internet connections and other problems. Support staff are responsible for the financial side of the company.

Most of the technical work at an Internet service provider is office work.

The Internet cafe

People who want to use the Internet, but do not have their own computer, can go to businesses that offer access to computers. They are called Internet cafés. How much the users pay depends on how long they use the Internet. Travelers all around the world use Internet cafés to stay in touch with friends and family at home.

The people who work at an Internet café know about computers and the Internet, so they can help customers find what they are looking for.

An Internet café

Website designers

Each Website on the World Wide Web has been created by a Website designer using special software or computer language, such as html. Each Website needs to be well laid out, so it is easy for people surfing the Web to find information on the site.

Graphic designers

There are many visual designs, called graphics, on Websites. These are produced by graphic designers. The graphic designer uses a computer to create eye-catching images and page layouts that will attract people to a Website. With so many Websites out there, it is important to make yours stand out from the rest.

A graphic designer chooses a color to use on a Website.

Internet teachers

The Internet is a very new medium, and people need skills to use it effectively. Some teachers run classes to teach people to use the Internet. They teach in many locations, such as big companies, schools, and community centers, in cities and country towns.

An Internet teacher gives a training class.

11

FROM IDEA TO WEBSITE

Every Website begins with an idea. This is the first stage in creating a functional Website. After the idea has been developed, there are several other important stages to go through before the Website is available on the World Wide Web. The stages on the flow chart below show how a Website is created. What goes on a Website and what it looks like depends on what the creator wants to achieve.

A Website

Stage 1 — IDEAS

Ideas for Websites come from all kinds of people. They could be based on people's age group, business interests, or hobbies.

Stage 2 — PLANNING AND RESEARCH

A Website needs planning and research before it can be developed and designed. The aim of the Website mostly determines what will appear on it. This is decided before the designing starts.

Stage 3 — WEBSITE DESIGN

Designing a Website is a creative process. Decisions are made about style and color, and about where information should be placed.

Website case studies

Read the five stages from idea to Website on pages 14–23 for three different Website case studies:

CASE STUDY 1
A family tree on the Web

CASE STUDY 2
A training Website

CASE STUDY 3
Selling photographs online

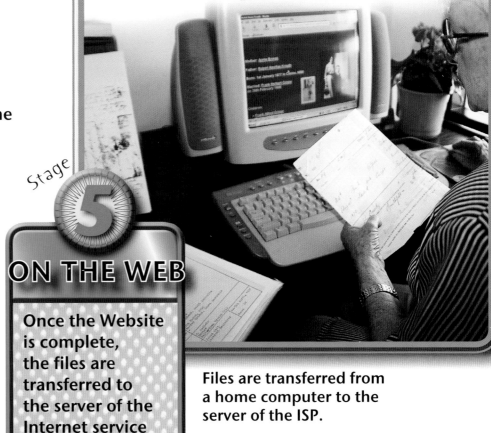

Stage 4
CHECKING

A Website needs to be checked before it is put on the Internet. It needs to be checked to make sure that all the links and other parts work the way they are designed to.

Stage 5
ON THE WEB

Once the Website is complete, the files are transferred to the server of the Internet service provider. The Website becomes part of the World Wide Web and everyone can access it.

Files are transferred from a home computer to the server of the ISP.

There are Websites on almost every possible topic in the world today. They come from a great range of sources, including huge companies with large computer departments, small businesses, and people at home with a hobby they wish to tell the world about.

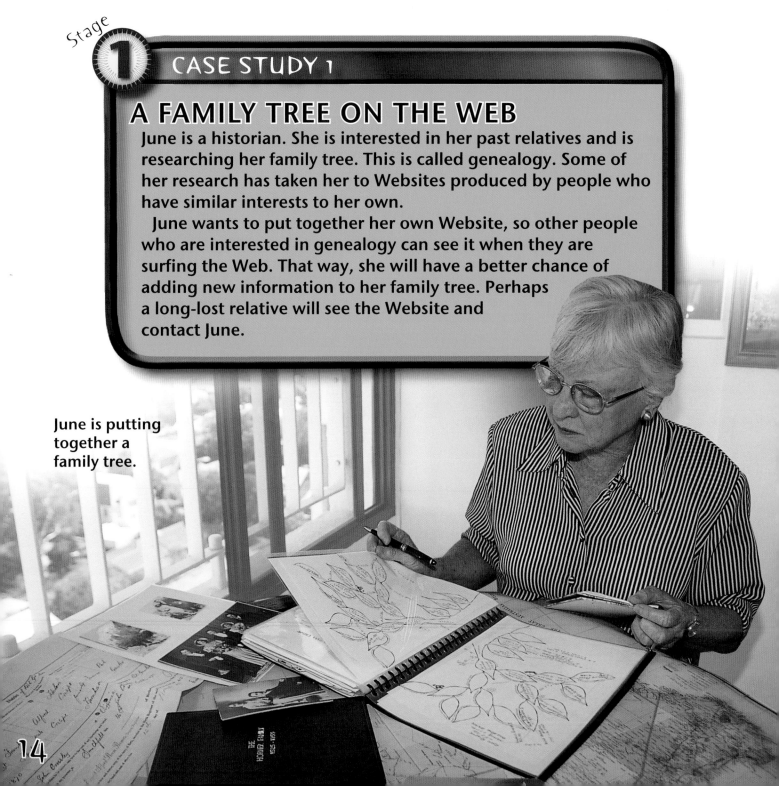

Stage

1

CASE STUDY 1

A FAMILY TREE ON THE WEB

June is a historian. She is interested in her past relatives and is researching her family tree. This is called genealogy. Some of her research has taken her to Websites produced by people who have similar interests to her own.

June wants to put together her own Website, so other people who are interested in genealogy can see it when they are surfing the Web. That way, she will have a better chance of adding new information to her family tree. Perhaps a long-lost relative will see the Website and contact June.

June is putting together a family tree.

CASE STUDY 2

A TRAINING WEBSITE

Some people do not have access to a class to learn about the Internet because they live in remote areas, away from big cities. Terry and Angela travel the Australian countryside to offer a course that is specially designed for rural people.

Terry has decided to produce a Website to use in the training. It will have **links** to Websites that interest country people, such as weather and farming sites. The students can still use the Website after Angela and Terry have left.

Terry and Angela drive to country areas to teach people how to use the Internet.

CASE STUDY 3

SELLING PHOTOGRAPHS ONLINE

Today, many businesses have Websites to show their products to customers. People can do their banking, pay bills, and shop on the Internet. Ellen, a photographer, wants a Website to advertise her photographs internationally. People who are looking for particular images will be able to find photographs and buy them on her Website.

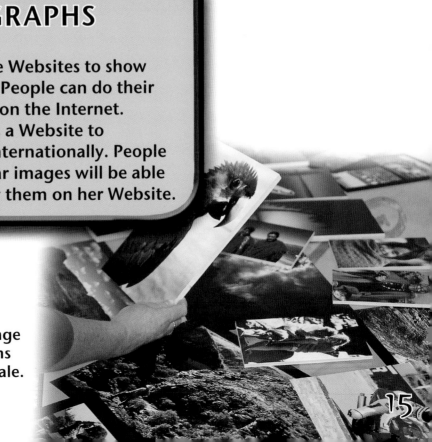

Ellen has a range of photographs available for sale.

2 PLANNING AND RESEARCH

Before setting up a Website, the person who designs it must understand what the main purpose of the site is and who will be using it. This information is vital, because it determines which features the Website should have. Researching other similar Websites gives a guide as to what sorts of features will be most useful. The Website designer needs this information to plan the Website.

Stage

CASE STUDY 1

A FAMILY TREE ON THE WEB

June's family tree is a complicated overview of all her relatives, going back to the 1700s. The information comes from many sources, such as other relatives and church and government records. June has visited lots of genealogy Websites to find the information. She has studied their layout to see how easy it is to use them. Now June writes down what needs to go on her own Website.

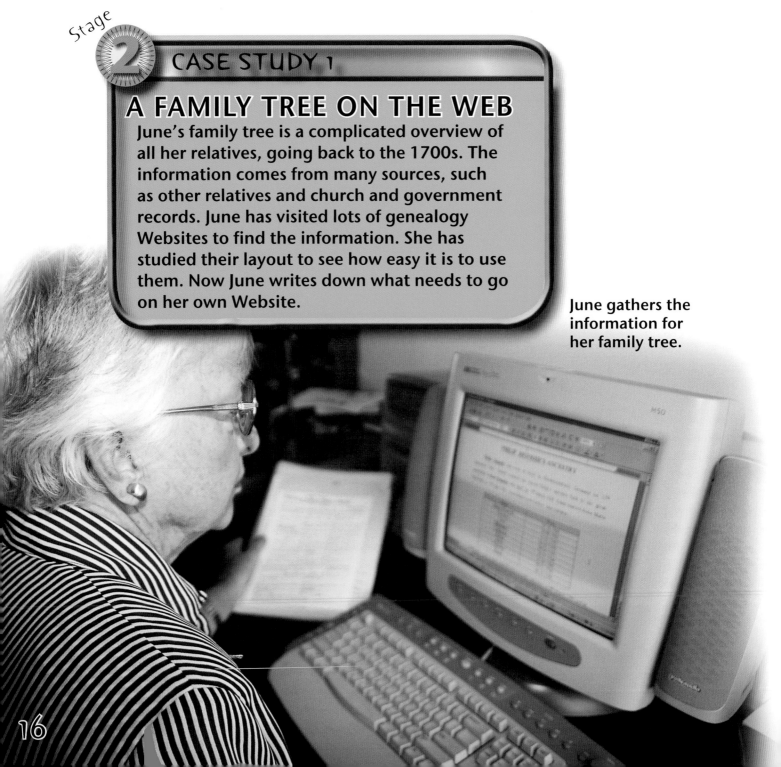

June gathers the information for her family tree.

CASE STUDY 2

A TRAINING WEBSITE

Terry searches the World Wide Web to find Websites that he thinks are interesting for people living in remote areas. He will put links to these Websites on his own Website. Farmers need information such as weather reports and wheat or wool prices. Often, there is no bank in the nearest town, so they might use Internet banking. Also, it takes time for newspapers to reach some remote areas, so some country people read them online.

Relevant Websites on the World Wide Web

CASE STUDY 3

SELLING PHOTOGRAPHS ON LINE

Ellen meets with Eva, a Website designer, to discuss the Website. Eva asks what the Website will be used for and what types of features Ellen needs. She also asks who will be looking at the Website, because that will determine the style of the site. Some of Ellen's photographs will be shown on the Website. They will be displayed in **low resolution**. This stops people from taking them from the Website and using them without paying. The Website will also run more quickly with small graphics. Ellen and Eva decide that an e-mail newsletter will be sent out regularly to inform people about new photographs on the Website.

Ellen meets with a Website designer to discuss her Website.

Website design is both an artistic and a technological process. A design brief says something about the Website's colors, layout, features, and graphics, and also includes a "map" of the site. The information for the Website is divided up into individual Webpages, which have links to the other pages of the Website and to other Websites.

The background design of a Website is known as the "skin." The Website can be designed using special computer software or by writing the design in computer code.

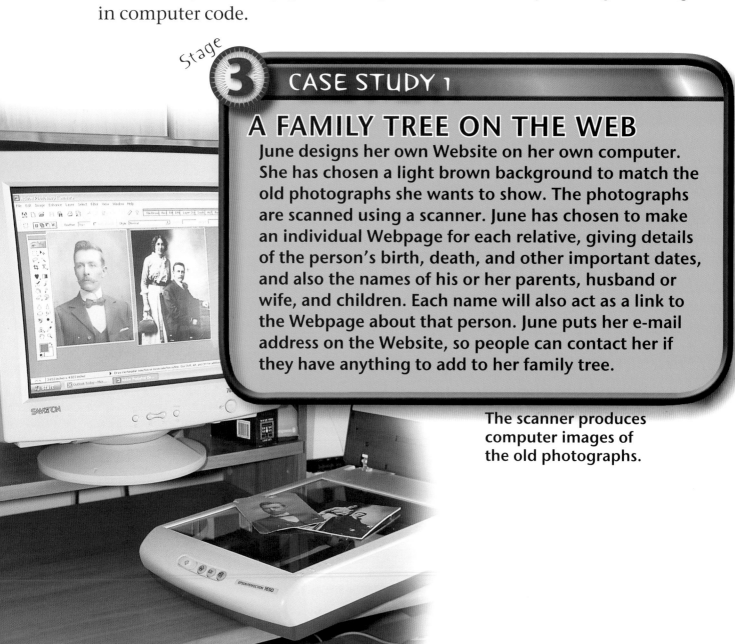

Stage

3

CASE STUDY 1

A FAMILY TREE ON THE WEB

June designs her own Website on her own computer. She has chosen a light brown background to match the old photographs she wants to show. The photographs are scanned using a scanner. June has chosen to make an individual Webpage for each relative, giving details of the person's birth, death, and other important dates, and also the names of his or her parents, husband or wife, and children. Each name will also act as a link to the Webpage about that person. June puts her e-mail address on the Website, so people can contact her if they have anything to add to her family tree.

The scanner produces computer images of the old photographs.

Stage

3

CASE STUDY 2

A TRAINING WEBSITE

Terry designs his Website for country people to start from while they are still learning to use the Internet. He makes easy links to the Websites he has found. He also puts in contact links, so the people can e-mail Terry and Angela if they need help after the course is over. The Website includes a booking form for people who want to take a training course in the future. Terry will update the Website regularly with the course timetable and other news.

Terry uses a computer code called html to design his Website.

Stage

3

CASE STUDY 3

SELLING PHOTOGRAPHS ONLINE

Eva creates a Website design brief, based on her discussion with Ellen. Then Eva and Alyssa, the graphic designer, create the skin together. It includes the logo and colors of Ellen's company. Eva uses special software to design the Website. She scans Ellen's photographs and adds them to the site. Some photographs will be changed regularly, to keep the Website interesting.

Alyssa creates the visual details for Ellen's Website.

4 CHECKING

Before a Website is made available on the World Wide Web, the designer must check that all links and features work properly. Each link is clicked on systematically to make sure the correct page appears each time. A Website with links that do not work properly is very annoying for users.

Stage 4 CASE STUDY 1

A FAMILY TREE ON THE WEB

June clicks on all the links on her Website to make sure they lead to the right Webpages. When she finds a problem, she goes back to the code that makes up the Website and corrects it. She has a book that tells her what to look for and how to fix it. June also makes sure that the right photos are shown for each person in her family tree.

June adjusts the code for her Website to correct a link.

Stage 4 CASE STUDY 2

A TRAINING WEBSITE

Terry goes over his Website, making sure all the links and contact details are correct. He also asks Angela to use the Website as if she were a customer. She looks at the pages in a different order from Terry. Angela double-checks the links and tells Terry where he has missed anything.

Terry will make changes to the Website regularly. He will check that the Website works each time he and Angela start a course in a country town.

Terry does a last-minute check on the Website while Angela sets up laptops for a training session.

CASE STUDY 3

SELLING PHOTOGRAPHS ONLINE

Eva checks the Website she has designed for Ellen. She goes over all the links and makes sure that the graphics are in the right places. Because customers will be entering their name, address, and credit card number on the Website, it is very important that it is **secure** and works properly. Eva sends Ellen a preview of the Website to make sure she is happy with the result.

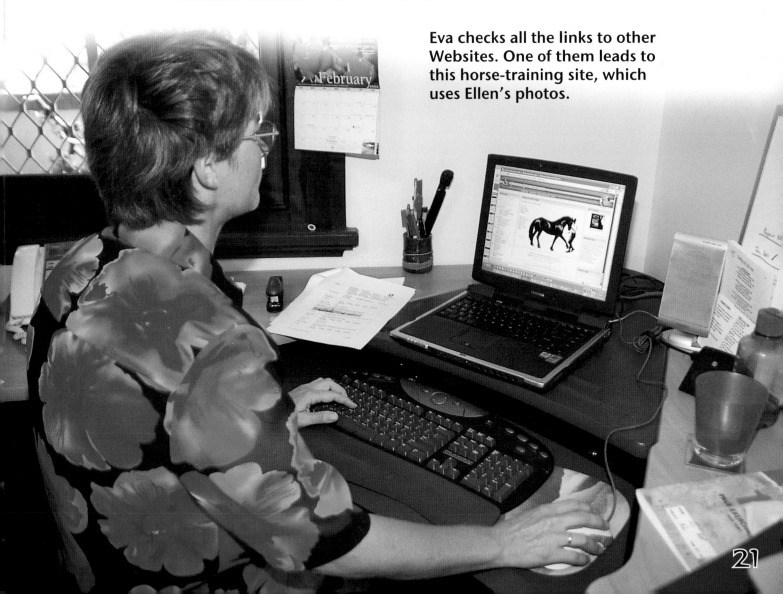

Eva checks all the links to other Websites. One of them leads to this horse-training site, which uses Ellen's photos.

21

5 ON THE WEB

To make a Website available to the public, all the files that make up the Website are transferred to a server. Big companies often have their own servers. Smaller companies and other people use a server at an Internet service provider.

Once the Website is "live," people surfing the Web can access it. They can type the domain name (URL) into their browser, or use a search engine to search for the topic or Website name.

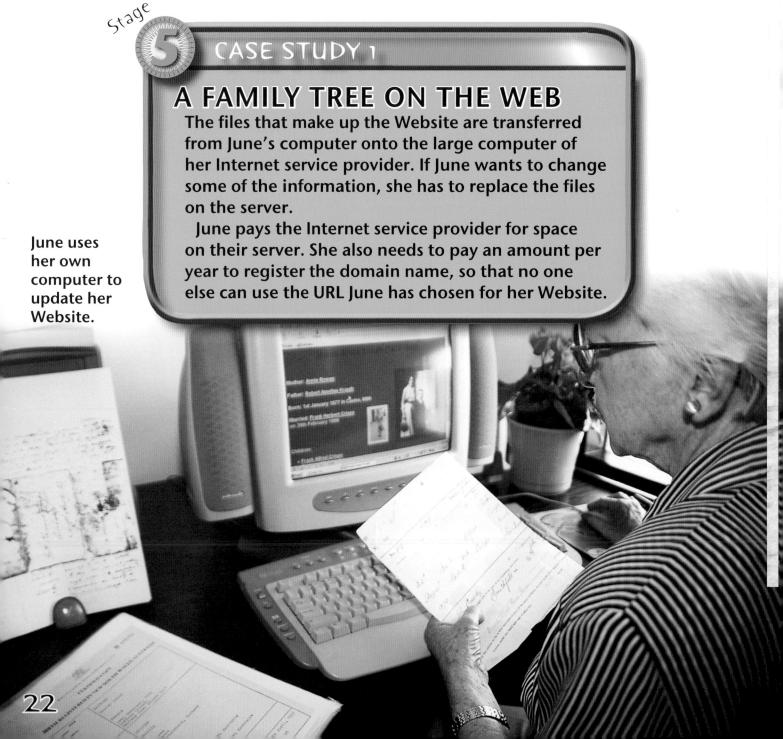

Stage

5 CASE STUDY 1

A FAMILY TREE ON THE WEB

The files that make up the Website are transferred from June's computer onto the large computer of her Internet service provider. If June wants to change some of the information, she has to replace the files on the server.

June pays the Internet service provider for space on their server. She also needs to pay an amount per year to register the domain name, so that no one else can use the URL June has chosen for her Website.

June uses her own computer to update her Website.

CASE STUDY 2

A TRAINING WEBSITE

Terry's Website is now on the server, so everyone with access to the Web can use it. Angela and Terry use the Website during their course. They project it onto a screen and show new Internet users how it works and where they should click. Angela uses the links to go to other Websites, such as the Internet-banking practice Website. Angela and Terry set up many laptops for each course. One computer is connected to the Internet and all the others are linked to it. This way, the students can all practice using the Internet.

Angela teaches a class using the Website designed by Terry.

CASE STUDY 3

SELLING PHOTOGRAPHS ONLINE

Ellen's Website is now part of the World Wide Web. When someone uses a search engine to look for photographs, her Website will be one of the thousands that come up. Ellen lets her customers know about the Website. Eva has set up the Website so that Ellen can make changes whenever she wants. Ellen adds new photographs every month. Updating a Website shows customers that the business is interested in its clients.

Ellen decides which photos to add to her Website.

23

DELIVERING THE MESSAGE

The access of the general public to the Internet depends on some complex technological equipment. At the moment, to use the Internet, you need a computer with a modem and access to a telephone line or other connection, such as cable.

The computer may be a full-size desktop computer, or a smaller laptop or palmtop computer. Some mobile phones offer Internet access as well.

A desktop computer connected to a house telephone line

A laptop connected to a mobile phone

A modem translates the information on the computer into signals that can be sent through the connection line. At the other end, the modem of the receiving computer translates the signals back into information the computer can understand. Many laptop and palmtop computers have a modem that is built in.

The telephone line can be a normal house telephone line or a special **digital** computer line. A normal telephone line is usually made of copper cable, but this technology is changing over to **fiber-optic cable**. Mobile phones can also be used to transmit e-mail and to connect to the World Wide Web.

Connections

For a dial-up connection, the modem dials the Internet service provider's phone number to gain access to the Internet. Usually, the computer only stays connected for a limited time. A dial-up connection provides the slowest form of access to the Internet.

Broadband connections are also called "digital subscriber lines" (DSL). They use new digital technology to transmit the information over more channels, so that many messages can be sent down one normal telephone line. A digital connection allows constant access to the Internet, so the user does not need to dial up each time to connect. It is also much faster than a dial-up connection.

Satellites and special fiber-optic cables provide other forms of Internet connections. They make it possible for many computers to use one connection at high speed. With a satellite connection, the information is sent via satellites that move around the Earth in space. Fiber-optic cables can carry information at an extremely high speed with very few errors.

A satellite dish sends and receives signals to and from a satellite in space.

INTERNET CAREERS

Many people who work with the Internet have learned computer skills at a university or college. Some are self-taught.

Eva is a Website designer

Eva plans a Website.

"I learned about the Internet and how to design Websites in one of my jobs for a big company. I decided to start my own business designing Websites for other people. I talk with the clients and find out what they want to use the Website for. From there, I design a Website to suit their needs."

Alyssa is a graphic designer

Graphic designer Alyssa

"I learned how to be a graphic artist by doing a degree in the subject at university. I work for a company that puts together graphics for home and contents pages on clients' Websites."

Patrick works at an Internet service provider

Patrick talks to a customer about a computer problem.

"I trained at university in Information Technology and got a job with an Internet service provider. When people call up with questions or problems, I work with them over the phone to fix the problem. It is a service we provide for customers of the ISP."

Mike runs an Internet café

"I always enjoyed the Internet and computers and I love meeting a variety of new people, so I started an Internet café. This one is very busy because it is in a tourist area. Travelers come here to go on the Internet so they can keep in touch with their friends and family back home."

Mike using one of the computers at the Internet café

Terry and Angela are Internet teachers

"When the Internet first started, we could see how useful it was. It became a hobby, and before long, we were training other people in how to use it. We also realized how useful the Internet would be for people in the country to access information about the weather and to do their shopping and banking. Now we travel the country, teaching farmers and people in country towns how to surf the Web."

Terry and Angela outside their motor home

INTERNET AND SOCIETY

The Internet is growing quickly. It reaches millions of people around the world.

Research

The Internet has revolutionized the way we can do research. Not long ago, books were our only source of information. Now we also have many Websites at our fingertips. Because anyone can put a website on the World Wide Web, the information is not always correct. If you use the Internet to research a subject, you also need to use other sources to make sure the information is accurate.

The *Encyclopedia Britannica* used to be in book form only. Now the information can also be found on the Web.

Business

Many banks offer online banking.

Many companies have Websites where they advertise and sell their products. This is called electronic business (e-business). It can save customers money and time, as they can book airfares and accommodation, order food, and pay bills online. Customers have to enter their credit card details, so great care is needed to make sure the company is honest.

Some companies send out unwanted e-mails advertising their products. These messages are annoying and take up space in our inboxes. They are called spam or junk mail.

Entertainment

On the Internet we can play games with people we have never met, from almost any part of the world. We can share information about our hobbies and chat with people who have similar interests.

The Internet makes it possible to download music and software. This has led to the development of illegal Websites, selling pirated software and music. When pirated products are sold, the people who created the music or software do not receive any money for their work.

Communication

E-mail and chatting have changed our methods of communication. Letters are becoming more and more rare as the faster electronic mail takes over.

Internet safety

Some people put racist material and sex Websites on the Internet. Many of these are illegal. The police try to find the people who are responsible, and try to stop them.

Viruses

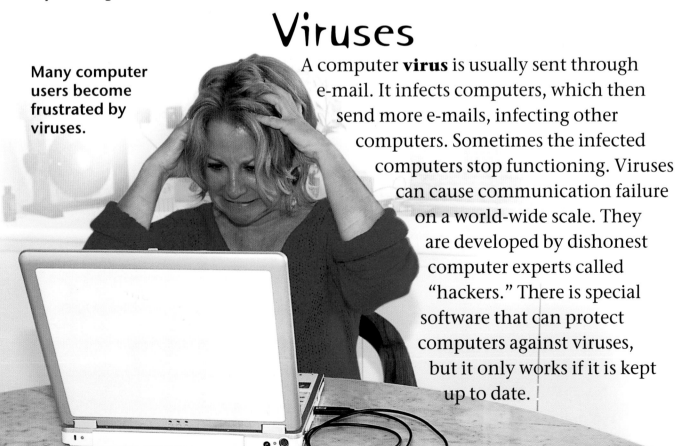

Many computer users become frustrated by viruses.

A computer **virus** is usually sent through e-mail. It infects computers, which then send more e-mails, infecting other computers. Sometimes the infected computers stop functioning. Viruses can cause communication failure on a world-wide scale. They are developed by dishonest computer experts called "hackers." There is special software that can protect computers against viruses, but it only works if it is kept up to date.

THE FUTURE OF THE INTERNET

It has been over 30 years since the Internet was first presented. Then, personal computers for the home did not exist. Today, nearly every household in the developed world has at least one computer, and many have Internet access. Connections are changing from dial-up to faster broadband. What will the next steps be?

A SMART FRIDGE

There are already computers in some refrigerators. Soon they will be able to detect which groceries are running low, and automatically e-mail a shopping list to a supermarket for home delivery.

LONG-DISTANCE DOCTORS

Doctors use e-mail technology to help people with health problems in remote areas. Using Internet cameras, specialists in a big-city hospital can see patients in the country. Even operations can be directed from a distance.

SPACE MAIL

We can e-mail people in remote places, such as a base in Antarctica. Perhaps in the future we will communicate with scientists in space stations, or even on other planets.

The Internet and other media

Other media—such as newspapers, magazines, photography, and radio—are available on the Web. Will the Internet replace these older forms of media one day?

Are these media on their way out?

GLOSSARY

developed world   modern countries that use new technologies

digital   carrying electronic information using numbers

domain names   the strings of letters that identify Websites on the Internet

download   to transfer information onto a computer

fiber-optic cable   a fine cable, made of glass or plastic, through which information is sent as short bursts of light

files   documents on a computer

Internet service provider (ISP)   a company with big computers providing access to the Internet

links   parts of a Website that, when they are clicked on, take the viewer to another Webpage

low resolution   made up of few colored dots, so the image is not clear when it is made bigger

modem   a piece of equipment that turns information on a computer into a signal that can travel over a telephone line and back

online   connected to the Internet

real time   happening at this time; live

secure   safe and well-protected for using personal details

server   a large computer that provides access to the Internet

software   the programs that run on computers

surf the Web   to look at Websites on the World Wide Web

virus   a program designed to disrupt computer functioning

INDEX